FARMER DUCK

RE-PLAYED BY
VIVIAN FRENCH

FROM THE BOOK BY
MARTIN WADDELL AND HELEN OXENBURY

WALKER BOOKS
AND SUBSIDIARIES

LONDON • BOSTON • SYDNE

First published 2000 by Walker Books Ltd
87 Vauxhall Walk, London SE11 5HJ

2 4 6 8 10 9 7 5 3 1

Playscript © 2000 Vivian French
Original text © 1991 Martin Waddell
Illustrations © 1991 Helen Oxenbury

This book has been typeset in Stempel Schneidler.

Printed in Singapore

British Library Cataloguing in Publication Data
A catalogue record for this book is
available from the British Library.

ISBN 0-7445-7267-3

Notes for Children

Farmer Duck is the story of a
very hard-working duck and a very lazy farmer.
You may know the story already, but it doesn't
matter if you don't.

This book is a little different from other picture books.
You will be sharing it with other people and telling
the story together.

You can read

this line

this line

this line

or this line.

Even when someone else is reading, try to follow
the words. It will help when it's your turn!

There once was a duck

Who had the bad luck

To live with a lazy old farmer.

The duck did the work.

The farmer stayed all day in bed.

All day?

Every day?

All day and every day.

The duck fetched the cow from the field.

The cow was in the rain.

The cold wet rain.

I can see the farmer.

The farmer's in the house.

The warm dry house.

What did the farmer say?

"How goes the work?" called the farmer.

The duck answered,

"Quack!"

The duck brought the sheep from the hill.

The sheep was very cold.

Very very cold.

"How goes the work?" called the farmer.

The duck answered,

"Quack!"

The duck put the hens in their house.

"How goes the work?" called the farmer.

The duck answered,

"Quack!"

Where's the farmer now?

The farmer's in his bed!

The farmer got fat through staying in bed

And the poor duck got fed up

With working all day.

All day every day!

"How goes the work?"

"Quack!"

The duck did the digging.

The duck did the sawing.

The farmer got fatter

And fatter

And fatter!

"How goes the work?"

"Quack!"

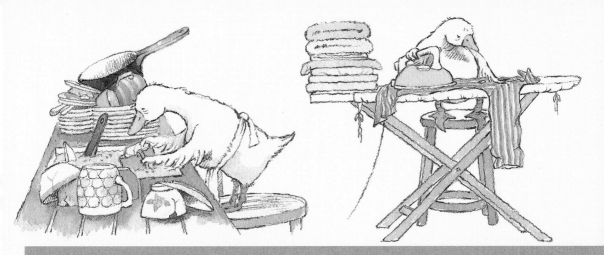

"How goes the work?"

"Quack!"

The duck did the dishes.

The duck did the ironing.

The farmer got fatter

And fatter

And fatter!

"How goes the work?"

"Quack!"

The duck climbed the ladder

And picked all the apples.

"How goes the work?"

"Quack!"

The duck fetched the eggs

And carried them home.

The farmer did nothing.

The farmer got fatter.

Fatter and fatter.

"How goes the work?"

"Quack!"

The poor duck was sleepy

And weepy

And tired.

The hens

And the cow

And the sheep

Got very upset.

They loved the duck.

So they held a meeting

Under the moon

And they made a plan

For the morning.

"Moo!"

Said the cow.

"Baa!"

Said the sheep.

"Cluck!"

Said the hens.

And *that* was the plan!

It was just before dawn

And the farmyard was still.

Through the back door

And into the house

Crept the cow

And the sheep

And the hens.

Shh!

Shh!

Shh!

Shh!

They stole down the hall.

They creaked up the stairs.

They squeezed under the bed of the farmer

And wriggled about.

The bed started to rock

And the farmer woke up,

And he called,

"How goes the work?"

And...

"Moo!"

"Baa!"

"Cluck!"

They lifted his bed

And he started to shout,

And they banged

And they bounced

The old farmer about

And about and about,

Right out of the bed...

And he fled

With the cow

And the sheep

And the hens

Mooing

And baaing

And clucking around him.

Moo!

Moo!

Baa!

Baa!

Cluck!

Cluck!

Down the lane…

"Moo!"

Through the fields…

"Baa!"

Over the hill…

"Cluck!"

And he never came back.

Never?

Never.

He never came back again.

The duck awoke

And waddled wearily into the yard

Expecting to hear, "How goes the work?"

But nobody spoke!

Then the cow

And the sheep

And the hens came back.

"Quack?" asked the duck.

"Moo!" said the cow.

"Baa!" said the sheep.

"Cluck!" said the hens.

Which told the duck the whole story.

Then mooing

And baaing

And clucking

And quacking

"Moo!"

"Baa!"

"Cluck!"

"Quack!"

They all set to work on their farm.

Notes for Teachers

Story Plays are written and presented in a way that encourages children to read aloud together. They are dramatic versions of memorable and exciting stories, told in strongly patterned language which gives children the chance to practise at a vital stage of their reading development. Sharing stories in this way makes reading an active and enjoyable process, and one that draws in even the reticent reader.

The story is told by four different voices, divided into four colours so that each child can easily read his or her part. The blue line is for more experienced readers; the red line for less experienced readers. When there are more than four children in a group, there is an ideal opportunity for paired reading. Partnering a more experienced reader with a less experienced one can be very supportive and provides a learning experience for both children.

Story Plays encourage children to share in the reading of a whole text in a collaborative and interactive way. This makes them perfect for group and guided reading activities. Children will find they need to pay close attention to the print and punctuation, and to use the meaning of the whole story in order to read it with expression and a real sense of voice.

The Big Book version can be used to introduce children to *Story Plays* in shared reading sessions. The class can be divided into groups to take part in reading the text aloud together, creating a lively performance.